Phonics Friends

Fatima and Fay
Find a Bird
The Sound of **F**

The Child's World

By Joanne Meier and Cecilia Minden

The Child's World

Published in the United States of America
by The Child's World®
PO Box 326
Chanhassen, MN 55317-0326
800-599-READ
www.childsworld.com

The Child's World®: Mary Berendes, Publishing Director

Editorial Directions, Inc.: E. Russell Primm, Editorial
Director and Project Editor; Katie Marsico, Associate
Editor; Judith Shiffer, Associate Editor and School Media
Specialist; Linda S. Koutris, Photo Researcher and
Selector

The Design Lab: Kathleen Petelinsek, Design and Page
Production

Photographs ©: BrandX: 12, 14; Corbis/Lynda
Richardson: 6; Corbis/Scott T. Smith: 18; Corbis/
Thomas Brummett: 8; Dwight Kuhn Photography: 16;
Getty Images/The Image Bank/Stephen Marks: cover,
4, 20; Getty Images/Taxi/Chabruken: 10.

Library of Congress Cataloging-in-Publication Data
Meier, Joanne D.
  Fatima and Fay find a bird : the sound of F / by Joanne
Meier and Cecilia Minden.
    p. cm. — (Phonics friends)
  Summary: Simple text featuring the consonant F, Fatima
and Fay find an injured bird, which they take to Dr. Fem.
  ISBN 1-59296-293-9 (library bound : alk. paper) [1.
English language—Phonetics. 2. Reading.] I. Minden,
Cecilia. II. Title. III. Series.
  PZ7.M5148Fat 2004
  [E]—dc22   2004001701

Note to parents and educators:
The Child's World® has created Phonics Friends with the goal of exposing children to engaging stories and pictures that assist in phonics development. The books in the series will help children learn the relationships between the letters of written language and the individual sounds of spoken language. This contact helps children learn to use these relationships to read and write words.

The books in this series follow a similar format. An introductory page, to be read by an adult, introduces the child to the phonics feature, or sound, that will be highlighted in the book. Read this page to the child, stressing the phonic feature. Help the student learn how to form the sound with her mouth. The Phonics Friends story and engaging photographs follow the introduction. At the end of the story, word lists categorize the feature words into their phonic element. Additional information on using these lists is on The Child's World® Web site listed at the top of this page.

Each book in this series has been carefully written to meet specific readability requirements. Close attention has been paid to elements such as word count, sentence length, and vocabulary. Readability formulas measure the ease with which the text can be read and understood. Each Phonics Friends book has been analyzed using the Spache readability formula. For more information on this formula, as well as the levels for each of the books in this series please visit The Child's World® Web site.

Reading research suggests that systematic phonics instruction can greatly improve students' word recognition, spelling, and comprehension skills. The Phonics Friends series assists in the teaching of phonics by providing students with important opportunities to apply their knowledge of phonics as they read words, sentences, and text.

This is the letter *f*.

In this book, you will read words that have the *f* sound as in:

   fish, five, food, and *four*.

This is Fatima and Fay.

They are five.

Fatima and Fay find a bird.

"Why can't the bird fly?"
asks Fay.

"His wing is hurt," says Fatima.
"We can help the bird."

"Let's find a safe place for the bird to rest," says Fay.

"We will take the bird to the doctor. Dr. Fem can fix the bird," says Fatima.

Fatima and Fay find Dr. Fem.

She is feeding some fish.

"Can you help this bird?"
asks Fay.

"I will try. The bird must rest
for four days," says Dr. Fem.

"We will give him food and water. We will help him fly."

Fatima and Fay look at the bird.

"Don't worry, bird! Soon you

will fly far away."

"This bird is lucky to find

two friends like you!"

says Dr. Fem.

Fun Facts

Some fish can live longer than human beings. Rougheye rockfish are found in the Pacific Ocean. They can live to be more than 200 years old! While most fish live underwater, lungfish are able to survive in mud puddles. Lungfish have been around for more than 300 million years and live in Africa, South America, and Australia.

Most birds use their wings to fly, but certain birds such as penguins and ostriches don't fly at all! Some scientists believe that certain birds can fly at speeds of up to 200 miles (322 kilometers) per hour.

Activity

Fish Watching

If you are interested in fish, take a trip to your local aquarium. You'll probably be able to see many kinds of fish, as well as other interesting water animals. Some aquariums even have special presentations that allow visitors to watch the fish as they are being fed. If you have a fish tank of your own at home, keep a journal. In it, describe what the fish look like, how often you feed them, and how they are different from or similar to one another.

To Learn More

Books
About the Sound of F

Flanagan, Alice. *Four Fish: The Sound of F.* Chanhassen, Minn.: The Child's
World, 2000.

About Fish

Pfeffer, Wendy, and Holly Keller (illustrator). *What's It Like to Be a Fish?.* New
York: HarperCollins, 1996.

Pfister, Marcus, and J. Allison James (translator). *The Rainbow Fish.* New York:
North-South Books, 1992.

About Flying

Lin, Grace. *Olvina Flies.* New York: Henry Holt, 2003.

Schmidt, Norman. *Paper Birds That Fly.* New York: Sterling Publishing, 1996.

About Friends

Carle, Eric, and Kazuo Iwamura. *Where Are You Going? To See My Friend!.*
New York: Orchard Books, 2003.

Edwards, Julie Andrews, Emma Walton Hamilton, and Tony Walton
(illustrator). *Dumpy's Friends on the Farm.* New York: Hyperion, 2001.

Web Sites
Visit our home page for lots of links about the Sound of F:

http://www.childsworld.com/links.html

Note to Parents, Teachers, and Librarians: We routinely check our Web links to make
sure they're safe, active sites—so encourage your readers to check them out!

F Feature Words

Proper Names

Fatima

Fay

Fem

Feature Words in Initial Position

far

feeding

find

fish

five

fix

fly

food

for

four

friends

Feature Word in Final Position

safe

About the Authors

Joanne Meier, PhD, has worked as an elementary school teacher and university professor. She earned her BA in early childhood education from the University of South Carolina, and her MEd and PhD in education from the University of Virginia. She currently works as a literacy consultant for schools and private organizations. Joanne Meier lives with her husband Eric, and spends most of her time chasing her two daughters, Kella and Erin, and her two cats, Sam and Gilly, in Charlottesville, Virginia.

Cecilia Minden, PhD, directs the Language and Literacy Program at the Harvard Graduate School of Education. She is a reading specialist with classroom and administrative experience in grades K–12. She earned her PhD in reading education from the University of Virginia. Cecilia and her husband Dave Cupp enjoy sharing their love of reading with their granddaughter Chelsea.